Words to Know Before You Read

across

contest

measure

mixture

special

sprinkles

super

www.rourkeeducationalmedia.com

Edited by Precious McKenzie
Illustrated by Helen Poole
Art Direction and Page Layout by Renee Brady

Library of Congress PCN Data

Mud Pie Queen / Meg Greve
ISBN 978-1-61810-170-9 (hard cover) (alk. paper)
ISBN 978-1-61810-303-1 (soft cover)
Library of Congress Control Number: 2012936772

Rourke Educational Media
Printed in the United States of America,
North Mankato, Minnesota

rourkeeducationalmedia.com

customerservice@rourkeeducationalmedia.com • PO Box 643328 Vero Beach, Florida 32964

MUD PIE Queen

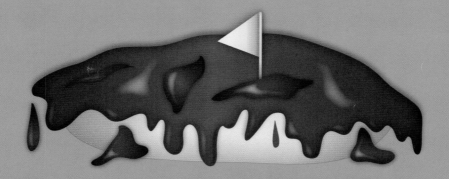

By Meg Greve

Illustrated by Helen Poole

Mudville is having a mud pie making contest.

The biggest pie will win.

Maddy makes her special, super, muddy mixture. Her mud pie is big.

Missy makes her special, super, muddy mixture.

She sprinkles it with grass.
Her mud pie is bigger.

Molly makes her special, super, muddy mixture. She adds more and more to her pie. Her mud pie is the biggest.

Who will win the contest?

"Let's measure the pies. We need a ruler," says Jill the judge.

They measure across Maddy's pie.
It is not so big.

They use inches to measure.

They measure Missy's pie. It is bigger.
They have to measure using the
whole ruler!

They measure Molly's BIG pie. "Get the yardstick!" says Jill the judge.

Molly is the mud pie queen
of Mudville!
Watch out!

21

After Reading Activities

You and the Story...

Why didn't Jill use the yardstick to measure Maddy's pie?

Who lost the contest? Why?

What were the units of measurement in this story? Put the units of measurement in order from smallest to biggest.

feet

inches

yards

Words You Know Now...

Each word is missing letters. Can you write the words on a piece of paper and fill in the missing letters?

acr___ ___s

c___ ___test

mea___ ___ ___ ___

m___ ___ture

___ ___ecial

spr___ ___ ___les

sup___ ___

You Could...Plan Your Own Mud Pie Contest

- Use a calendar to choose the best day for your contest. Make sure an adult says it is okay.

- Make some invitations inviting your friends to compete in the contest. Make sure the invitations tell:
  - About the contest.
  - When the contest takes place.
  - Where the contest takes place.
  - Everyone to wear clothes they can get muddy.

- Ask someone to be the judge and make sure the judge has measuring tools. You also need a prize for the winner.

- Find the perfect spot to make mud pies. Be sure you have buckets, water, and something to use to stir your special muddy mixture.

About the Author

Meg Greve lives in Chicago with her husband, daughter, and son. Her son LOVES to make really muddy mixtures in the backyard. Her daughter does not!

Ask The Author!
www.rem4students.com

Helen Poole lives in Liverpool, England, with her fiancé. Over the past ten years she has worked as a designer and illustrator on books, toys, and games for many stores and publishers worldwide. Her favorite part of illustrating is character development. She loves creating fun, whimsical worlds with bright, vibrant colors. She gets her inspiration from everyday life and has her sketchbook with her at all times as inspiration often strikes in the unlikeliest of places!